THE SCHIFF WHO CRIED WOLF... BLITZER

A. J. NEAL
PUBLISHING

Published by A.J. Neal Publishing
915 Bennetts Mills Road #1469
Jackson, NJ 08527

Illustrations: Shallu Narula
Copyediting: Lynette M. Smith
Cover design and interior layout: Damonza.com

Softcover print edition ISBN: 978-0-9851442-5-8
Electronic edition ISBN: 978-0-9851442-6-5

First Printing 2020
Printed in the United States of America

THE SCHIFF WHO CRIED WOLF... BLITZER

CHRISTOPHER HOLL

A. J. NEAL
PUBLISHING

To the deplorables

de·plor·a·ble

/dəˈplôrəb(ə)l/

Noun

1. hardworking American patriot

Once upon a time, in the Land of the Swamp, there lived a court jester known as the Schiff. He had the eyes of an owl and the neck of a pencil. Though just a fool, the Schiff dreamed of being part of the upper crust and ingratiated himself with political elites whenever the chance arose. It mattered not to him how he advanced—bold exaggerations, half-truths, and outright lies were his modus operandi, so long as they positioned him favorably with the ruling class.

Word of Jester Schiff's entertaining skills, particularly storytelling, coupled with his ambition, caught the ear of Her Highness, Queen Nanshee. The queen was a quite mature lady whose kingdom was perched high atop Caphill Mountain, overlooking the deplorable townspeople. She would give the Schiff an opportunity to prove himself worthy of being more than just a court jester. With two claps of her hands, she summoned him to her throne.

"At thy service, Your Highness," said the stooping jester upon entering her chamber.

Court Jester Schiff, a gifted storyteller

"King MAGA, my mortal enemy in the nexsht province, is becoming far too popular and powerful among his people. They've become proshperous; there is much variety and availability of food, drink, dress, and employ; he's built up quite an army too. How he became king, I'll never understand. Oh, how I despise those deplorables! Alas, what's done is done; but his reforms must not catch on with my indoctrinated subjects, or they may turneth on me."

"Yes, Your Highness, King MAGA is quite the rabble rouser."

"Twicesh, I sent soldiers into his territories to stir up trouble, even knocking down the walls of his fortress, and threatening to subsume his kingdom into mine; but each time, he just rebuilt the walls. "Build the walls, build the walls!" he would bellow after pushing my armies back. And the walls would be built. We seem powerless against King MAGA and his loyal followers. Is there anything that you, my evil-minded, bug-eyed, pencil-neck court jester, can do to breaketh the bond between him and his loyal MAGA crown-wearing followers?"

Queen Nanshee

I am quite shifty, thought the Schiff to himself. *This is mine chance. If I am successful in helping Queen Nanshee—no more fool's hat for me.*

"Your majesty, yes, there are things thou can do to breaketh that bond."

"Art thou sure? Those foolish bitter clingers cling so bitterly strong to King MAGA. And to their religion and crossbows. How will thee ever pull them apart?"

"Assign, malign, and undermine," said the Schiff. "Assign, malign, and undermine."

"Thou soundeth like Lord Jessejacks with all that rhyming. Now, tell me, what dost thou mean?"

"Assign. We assign dark motives to everything King MAGA does or wants to do. Create false narratives. Sow doubt and distrust among his followers. Slowly, his MAGA-matism wanes, as support for thee doth wax."

A maid servant entered the chamber and poured stouts of the swamp-brewed Mueller's Hard Ale for Queen Nanshee and the Schiff. "Perfect timing," said the queen, "it'sh Mueller time. Oh, how I love Mueller time," she slurred. Raising her cup, she toasted, "to our shuckshess."

"Yes, to our shuckshess… er, success," replied the Schiff as he gulped down the frothy liquid. "We cannot fail."

"What canst thou do?"

"Leaflet him."

"Leaflet him?"

"Yes," explained the Schiff. "We'll use that newfangled ink press of Earl Guttenberg, and print leaflets—hundreds of them, full of slanderous stories about King MAGA—and drop them all throughout the kingdom. The stories will be outrageous and salacious. It will not matter that the leaflet is not corroborated or verified because what is important is the seriousness of the charges, not whither they are true. His followers will not be able to support him once those stories start circulating about his kingdom."

"Ooh, that sounds splendid. And what name wilt thou givest this leaflet?"

"Yes, yes, your majesty. It needeth a name, for credibility. Hmm. I've got it. We'll call it the *New World Times*. Thee will have all the news that is unfit to print… about King MAGA."

"Magnificent. But, what if the lies, er, stories, by credible anonymous sources, of course, fail to create discord between King MAGA and his deplorable followers, as you suggest they wilst do?"

"I am sure it will work—but if it does not, we malign and accuse him of committing a high crime with Ms. Demeanor, that maiden of questionable character from the adjoining village. She doth have a stormy temper and scandalous reputation. Just the association with her will ruinith him."

"That should work, I guess. But… King MAGA is quite resilient. What if it does not?"

"Well, then we have to really fight—really go to battle."

"Surely, you joust… er, jest…Jester Schiff."

"This wilt be our last chance to truly undermineth King MAGA from his loyal subjects. He wilt be ugly. He shall wish to voluntarily abdicate the throne, of that I am sure."

"Yes, yes, tell me." Queen Nanshee asked excitedly, "What exactly wilt thou do?"

"We will peach him."

"Peach him?"

"Yes, peachest him."

"Pray tell, what dost thou mean?" asked the queen.

"Peach him. With a pie."

"And what will peaching him… with a pie… a peach pie—what will peaching, or pie-ing him, do?" asked Queen Nanshee.

"Dirty him up. Soil him. Cast doubt on him. I mean, if he is being peached, clearly, he hast done something wrong. It is not often that a king is peached—it almost never happens—so it must meaneth that he is guilty. Of something. Just punishment for unjust and cruel actions. His deplorables won't be able to stomach him any longer."

"He is very distasteful, I admit. But tell me, Jester Schiff," asked the queen, "What, exactly are King MAGA's unjust actions—which I am sure number many; but for the sake of time, just divulge a few, as I must get on with my important royal and prayerful duties."

"He, uh, he… I mean, he… uh… he hast… uh…, hast his own ideas, and his hair… uh, he is unlike us—an outsider, ignores our fiats…."

"Well, then, that's good enough for me. Go on, my pencil-necked friend, tell me more of thy plan," said Queen Nanshee.

"Once the peaching begins, King MAGA will be surprised and, more so, shocked, at our audacity. He'll be soiled and sticky and look like a fool. Even his most ardent supporters will turn away, and some will join the pie d'resistance—they will not think it futile. Subjects who remain loyal to him will dwindle in numbers and, over time, simply fade away—and so will he. The reign of this barbarian will finally be over."

"And he will be," said Queen Nanshee with smug satisfaction, "peached forever."

And so Jester Schiff put his plan into action. The salacious leaflet was disturbing, riddled with terrible transgressions about King MAGA; but, since it was all lies, it failed to turn his subjects against him. Without missing a beat, the Schiff then tried to frame King MAGA for a high crime with Ms. Demeanor. This too fell flat. Queen Nanshee became increasingly irritated and the Schiff worried about remaining a court jester forever. The time had come to peach King MAGA.

The Schiff sought advice from Sir Peter Struckstroke, a corrupt knight of Queen Nanshee's Knights of the Clown's Table. He was a former squire in the Feudal Bureau of Illusion—and past recipient of the 'Merlin Award' for outstanding sleight-of-hand skills. Sir Struckstroke thought loyalists of King MAGA were smelly.

"Take a page from me," suggested Sir Struckstroke, "and turn the page on the truth. Truth is overrated, unless telling it can benefit you. Otherwise, stayeth away from it—like the black plague. Take another page from the wealthy guilds, and always have an insurance policy on hand. And if it is a peaching you seek, enlist the assistance of Chef Nadler. He will eat it up."

Sir Peter Struckstroke, former squire in the Feudal Bureau of Illusion

Chef Nadler was an odd-looking figure and a bit of a hunchback, as he spent most of his days cooking for the castle, hunched over a big, boiling cauldron of pottage stew. The knight and the jester descended to the basement and found their way to the kitchen. They told the chef of their plans.

"Though hast come to the right gentleman to peach political enemies," said Chef Nadler to Schiff and Struckstroke as he leaned into the stew and took a sniff, stirring in a few additional spices. "I came close to doing it once myself. But… well, when I had that fresh-out-of-the-fireplace, piping hot, delicious peach pie in my fudgy little fingers… it, well… um… sort of… disappeared" he said nervously as his stomach growled. "But I promise it won't happen this time. I'll get busy right now and bake a whole pantry fulleth of peach pie."

Chef Nadler, able to cook up something from absolutely nothing

Jester Schiff and Sir Struckstroke found a few serfs suffering from MAGA Madness Malady who were all too eager to peach King MAGA. Pie d'resistance they called themselves. As luck would have it, King MAGA would be reviewing a grand military parade the day they planned to peach. Just the publicity they needed.

The parade was an impressive display of military prowess. Knights on horses and war elephants passed by the stands where nobles and King MAGA were seated. Next came foot soldiers, catapults, battering rams and flame throwers. Then archers marched by, fitted with crossbows and longbows, war hammers and battle axes. King MAGA looked on with respect, awe, and satisfaction.

Meanwhile, with peach pies hidden in their undergarments, the pie d'resistance blended in with the onlookers along the parade route. Jester Schiff had secretly appointed one of them as the whistleblower; at the opportune moment, with a quick blow of hot air into the woodwind instrument, he would sound the alarm—their signal to spring into action, advance on King MAGA, and peach him. He would be, as Queen Nanshee somberly and gleefully characterized, peached forever.

The whistleblower

But, as providence would have it, the peaching of King MAGA had the opposite effect. The more he was peached, the stronger he grew in resolve and in stature. His subjects became more emboldened and numerous. MAGA crowns dotted the landscape. Queen Nanshee was understandably concerned and became more incoherent and unhinged as the days passed.

"Schiff, Schiff... thou, thou... pencil-necked jester!" screamed the queen. "Look what thou hast done! Thou hast ruined me! My subjects' eyes have opened to the possibility that this kingdom mightest be great again. That bodes ill for me. I need peasants to need me and my little crumbs. And my prayerfulness. What are we going to do? More to the point, what wilt thou do? Thou may like to stretch the truth, Jester Schiff, but I like to stretch buffoons like you—on the rack!"

Trembling, the Schiff reassured Queen Nanshee that it was not over—yet. He had one last card to play. "Your Highness, there is still a chance we can control the minds of the peasants, so they believe what we want them to believe."

"Like what? Is there nothing left for you to do but seek help from The Shrew, that roundtable of anti-King MAGA, crooked-nosed crones led by Lady Joyless of Behar and the notorious Whooper of Goldberg who meet each morning and moan about everything MAGA while chanting 'Bubble, bubble, toil and trouble'? Not that there's anything wrong with that."

"Uh, no, not exactly, it is—"

"Jester Schiff," interrupted the queen. "Thou shouldst knowest that I have ordered the guards to prepare the rack—for you! So, this had better be good—or I will tear you apart. I'm good at tearing things apart, you know. What dost thou have in mind?"

"The town liar."

"The town liar?" asked the queen.

"Yes, the town liar, Sir Wolf Blitzer. He is just the one who can helpeth us now." The Schiff cried out, "Wolf. Wolf. *Wooooooooooooolf!*"

Dressed in a red and gold coat, breeches, black boots and a tricorne hat, Wolf, the town liar, ran up to the castle. "Ahh, Your Majesty, how may I be of service to you? Anything, anything. Please, let me do your bidding, whatever it is. Anything! Ahh!"

Jester Schiff interrupted. "Town liar Wolf, I need you to inform all the subjects of this and surrounding kingdoms that the stories in the *New World Times* about King MAGA are all 100 percent true, that he committed a high crime with Ms. Demeanor and that his peaching means he's unqualified to serve as king. Spread these lies, er, stories throughout the countryside using your network of King MAGA naysayers— the Countryside Naysayer Network, or CNN, as you call it. Got it?"

"Ahh, yes, of course, but were not all of those stories debunkedeth… by real debunkers?"

"Wolf! It doesn't matter. You just need to repeat, over and over and over and over and over and over and over and over and over and over and over and over again… the salacious stories and accusations. And then, repeat them over and over and over again. And then again once more. Sooner or later, they will sticketh. Like a peach pie."

"Here ye, Here ye, I doth have breaking news and a developingeth story"

But the lies did not stick. Wolf, the town liar, tried hard. His "Here ye, Here ye, I doth have breaking news and a developingeth story" and ringing of bells were heard all over the kingdom. For weeks… for months… and for years he repeated exactly, word for word, what Queen Nanshee and Jester Schiff told him to say. But for most fair-minded people, it was useless background noise, and no one payed much attention to it.

Over time, King MAGA's sensible reforms took hold and spread throughout the kingdoms, benefitting both serfs and royals alike. Queen Nanshee, Jester Schiff, and other political elites slowly died out because their only interest lay in accumulating more and more power for themselves, and not serving the good people with whom they were entrusted.

And the deplorables lived happily ever after.

You won't find a The End in this story—it's just the beginning

About the author

Christopher Holl is pretty much your typical American citizen—husband, father, worker, taxpayer, patriot. Believes in God, life, individual liberty, and the Second Amendment. Yeah, he's a deplorable.